POKÉMON
GALAR REGION
ACTIVITY BOOK

PIKACHU PRESS™

Pokémon Galar Region Activity book
$12.99 USA
$17.99 CAN

The Pokémon Company
INTERNATIONAL

Publisher: Heather Dalgleish
Sr. Publishing Manager: Mark Hughes
Art Director: Chris Franc
Design Manager: Hiromi Kimura
Designer: Justin Gonyea and Lauren Parra
Editors: Wolfgang Baur, Hollie Beg, Holly Bowen, and Stephen Crane
Sr. Consumer Product Approval Manager: Amy Ganster
Sr. Consumer Product Approval Associate: Hank Woon
Writer: Lawrence Neves

Dedicated to my awesome kids, Emily and Nicholas.
This book would not have happened without you.

The Pokémon Company International
10400 NE 4th Street, Suite 2800
Bellevue, WA 98004 USA

3rd Floor Building 10, Chiswick Park, 566 Chiswick High Road
London, W4 5XS United Kingdom

Retain these addresses for your records.

Printed in Huizhou, Guangdong, China.
First printing November 2020.

This book was produced by Quarto Publishing Group USA Inc.
ISBN: 978-1-60438-207-5

POKÉMON
GALAR REGION
ACTIVITY BOOK

WELCOME TO THE GALAR REGION

Welcome, Pokémon adventurers, to a brand-new activity book centered around the newest Pokémon region, Galar! You're going to find new puzzles, new quests—and maybe some new friends! You'll also meet some new and exciting never-before-seen Pokémon, so let's get our gear and head out!

POKÉMON HEIGHT AND WEIGHT CHART FOR THE GALAR REGION

This activity book occasionally refers to the height, weight, and type of particular Pokémon. Even an expert Trainer doesn't have them all memorized, of course, so you'll find a helpful reference card at the back of the book listing select Pokémon by name, with all that information included. Tear it out carefully along the perforations, and you can consult it any time you need to know details for these Pokémon that can be found in the Galar region!

BUILD 5 OF YOUR OWN PAPERCRAFT POKÉ BALLS!

Every Trainer should have their own collection of Poké Balls! It's easy to make the papercraft Poké Balls included with this book. Simply tear out each sheet carefully along the perforations. Follow the instructions to construct each Poké Ball, from the basic model up to an Ultra Ball and even a Master Ball!

GROOKEY'S CROSSWORD CHALLENGE

Grookey is having a hard time getting its pals sorted out—help Grookey find out more about its Pokémon friends by solving this Pokémon Crossword! We even started you off with a clue to help you and Grookey out!

ACROSS

5. This Pokémon has a body of sparkling gold. People say it no longer remembers that it was once human.

6. It swims along with a school of Remoraid, and they'll all fight together to repel attackers.

7. It wears a rag fashioned into a Pikachu costume to look less scary. Unfortunately, the effect only makes it creepier.

DOWN

1. Its resilient tusks are its pride and joy. It licks dirt to take in the minerals it needs to keep its tusks in top condition.

2. When it uses its special stick to strike up a beat, the sound waves carry revitalizing energy to the plants and flowers nearby.

3. It launches water bubbles with its legs, drowning prey within the bubbles. This Pokémon can then take its time to savor its meal.

4. This Pokémon haunts dilapidated mansions. It sways its arms to hypnotize opponents with the ominous dancing of its flames.

GROOKEY

6

IT TAKES ALL TYPES, MORPEKO

Morpeko is looking for similar Pokémon to hang with in Galar. Help Morpeko out by identifying any Pokémon below that match at least one of Morpeko's types (hint: It's an Electric- and Dark-type Pokémon!) Good luck!

MORPEKO

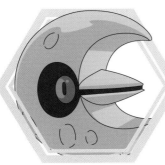

LUNATONE

ROCK-PSYCHIC

GOODRA

DARK

PURRLOIN

WATER

MANECTRIC

DRAGON

PICHU

ELECTRIC

KINGLER

SCORBUNNY

SCORBUNNY WORD JUMBLE

Scorbunny is running around and firing everyone up looking for another Pokémon! Help calm Scorbunny down by figuring out who the sought-after Pokémon might be! Unscramble these Pokémon, then enter them in order into the boxes below. Use the highlighted letter boxes to find the Pokémon that Scorbunny is looking for!

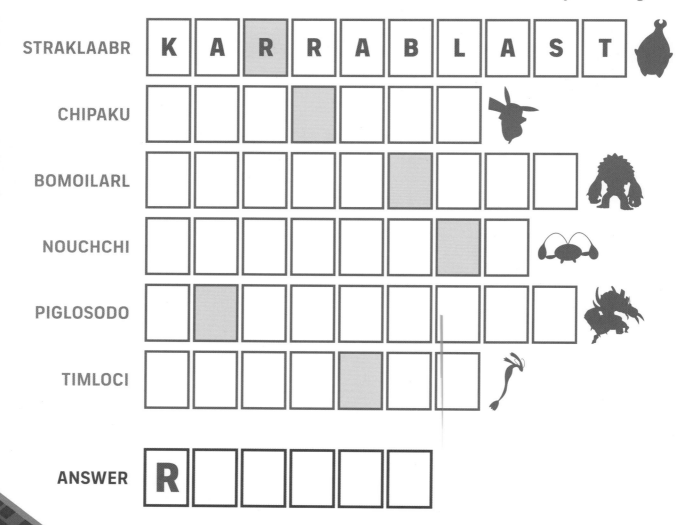

STRAKLAABR | K | A | R | R | A | B | L | A | S | T

CHIPAKU

BOMOILARL

NOUCHCHI

PIGLOSODO

TIMLOCI

ANSWER | R

SOBBLE'S POKÉMON CHECKLIST

Before we go much farther, let's train to see if you know anything about the Pokémon in the Galar region. Sobble is interested in knowing if you can name the following Pokémon with just these short clues, and a silhouette of their forms?

 Revealing the eyelike patterns on the insides of its ears unleashes its psychic powers. It normally keeps the patterns hidden, however.

_____

 This Pokémon eats trash, which it transforms into poison inside its body. The main component of the poison depends on what sort of trash was eaten._____

 It has an easygoing nature. It doesn't care if it bumps its head on boats and boulders while swimming.

_____

 It stores berries inside its shell. To avoid attacks, it hides beneath rocks and remains completely still. _____

 A warm-up of running around gets fire energy coursing through this Pokémon's body. Once that warm-up is complete, it's ready to fight at full power.

_____

 If a tree branch shakes when there is no wind, it's a _____, not a tree. It hides from the rain.

 By releasing enmity-erasing waves from its ribbonlike feelers, _____ stops any conflict.

ANSWERS ON PAGE 89 ▶

HOW MANY POKÉMON CAN YOU NAME?

Here's an exercise that will sharpen your skills as a Trainer. According to the Height and Weight Chart in the back of the book (after page 96), see how many of these questions you can answer based on Pokémon we've discovered so far!

INSTRUCTIONS

Take turns and play against a friend for a real challenge. You get one point for every right answer, but your opponent gets two points for every answer you missed! Be very careful!

1 How many Pokémon are under three feet tall? _____

2 How many Pokémon are dual-types? _____

3 How many Pokémon weigh 30 lbs. or over? _____

4 How many Pokémon have wings? _____

5 How many Pokémon stand on two feet? _____

6 How many Pokémon have Water-type in their types? (Dual-types count!) _____

7 Are there more Normal or Grass types in Pokémon? _____

SPOT THE DIFFERENCE WITH CORVIKNIGHT

It's hard not to notice Corviknight. Its impressive black steel luster can drive terror into any casual observer. But would you know Corviknight at first glance? Check out these Corviknight (and Corviknight imposters) and see if you can find the real Corviknight? Time yourself for a real challenge.

ANSWER ON PAGE 89 ▶

ODD POKÉMON OUT WITH WOOLOO

What curly-fleeced Pokémon is just begging to be hugged? That's right, it's Wooloo! But Wooloo likes to hang out with its friends—so let's find it some similar Pokémon for Wooloo to hang out with. See if you can identify other Pokémon from the group below that match Wooloo's type exactly. Play with a friend and time yourself!

SILICOBRA

SKWOVET

WINGULL

EEVEE

TYMPOLE

WAILORD

BUNNELBY

GREEDENT

QWILFISH

SNORLAX

12

ANSWERS ON PAGE 89 ▶

CRYPTOGLYPHICS

Can you figure out which Pokémon we might be talking about below? Decipher the clues below and use the cryptographic to solve this puzzle.

LEGEND

W   R   D   E   N   A

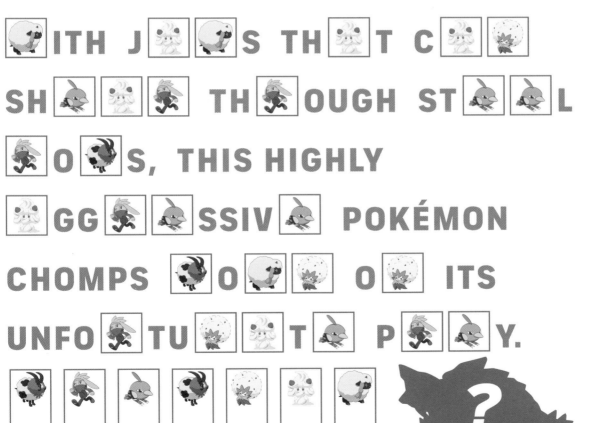

ITH J S TH T C

SH TH OUGH ST L

O S, THIS HIGHLY

GG SSIV POKÉMON

CHOMPS O O ITS

UNFO TU T P Y.

ANSWER ON PAGE 89 ▶

MAWILE

WORD SEARCH WITH MAWILE

Hey adventurer! See if you can find the following Pokémon in this list. Once you've circled all the Pokémon, use the red letters to spell out the missing Pokémon we're looking for. Good luck—and for an extra challenge, circle the red-lettered answers first, which will help spell out the name of the Pokémon.

MAWILE
BOLDORE
MILOTIC
MUDSDALE
CHEWTLE
PIDOVE
GASTRODON
GROOKEY
ONIX
VILEPLUME
THWACKEY
DREDNAW
NICKIT
BEWEAR
SCORBUNNY
SNORUNT
SOBBLE
SNOVER
LAPRAS

```
K Z K I S G A S T R O D O N P J O
T Y Y K J N C H E W T L E K I J M
L D O G R O O K E Y V Z I A D S P
J P J T X X U V A W T F M J O H J
X G A P P W H W E Z K H A U V M R
N I C K I T A O O R O W W B E A S
P Y J R P N I N Z S Y L I X E A T
A I V D D I N I U N S H L W R J T
Y N O E A D Q X N O C G E P L R H
A V R J L S B U B R B B A S A J W
B D T F G A B B A U V L K X A W A
L A N U U R O A O N M I L O T I C
B O L D O R E V I T W H E N B J K
A X X C V I L E P L U M E N Q R E
L I S A E N Z Q W M D Z I W G J Y
M U D S D A L E G A I H A C J I P
N X B Q R U F R E D O S O B B L E
```

The Pokémon we are looking for is ___ ___ ___ ___ ___ ___ ___ ___ ___ ___ ___ ___ ___

ANSWERS ON PAGE 89 ▶

WHO'S THAT POKÉMON? FEATURING CHEWTLE

Chewtle is a fascinating Pokémon. Apparently, its teething itch makes it snap its jaws at anything that gets too close. It also likes to attack with its horn. Let's see if you can identify these six other Pokémon that also have horns just like Chewtle.

1

2

3

4

5

6

ANSWERS ON PAGE 90 ▶

STEELIX

WEIGHT FOR IT WITH STEELIX

Okay, so you're getting the hang of it, adventurer. Let's see how you do with Pokémon weights.

From lightest to heaviest, can you put these Pokémon in order? Don't let their height fool you—some of these Pokémon are a lot denser than others! Use the Height and Weight Chart in the back of the book if you need some help!

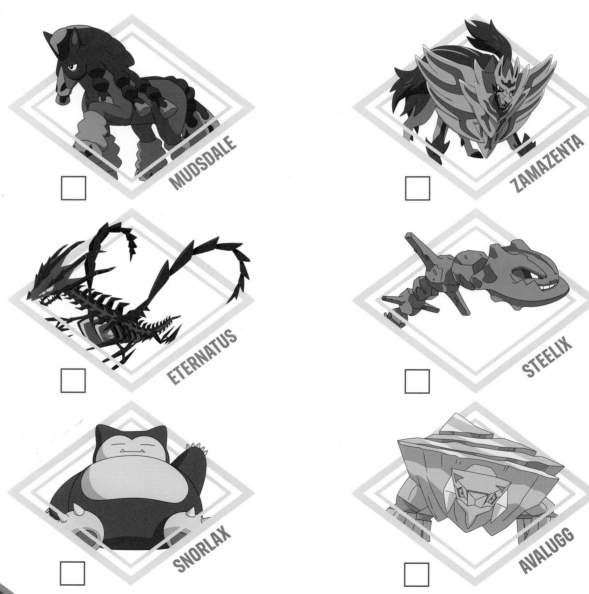

MUDSDALE

ZAMAZENTA

ETERNATUS

STEELIX

SNORLAX

AVALUGG

ANSWERS ON PAGE 90 ▶

RING AROUND THE COLORS WITH GOSSIFLEUR

If you're looking for a bright and beautiful Pokémon, Gossifleur checks all the boxes! But can you finish coloring this drawing below with the correct colors? We'll give you three choices, and without looking it up in the back of the book, see if you can color Gossifleur in with the correct combination!

Gossifleur uses shades of which colors?

ANSWERS ON PAGE 90 ▶

GREEDENT

SPOT THE DIFFERENCE WITH GREEDENT

Greedent is a furry, funny Pokémon with an adorable look and some amazing skills! Let's test your ability to recognize Greedent, and have a little fun along the way. In the page below are Greedent, along with two other Pokémon that share its type. When you find them, look closely to make sure you have exactly the right ones—we threw in some differences to see how sharp you are, adventurer! Good luck!

MAZE ME NICKIT!

Nickit is cunning and cautious, and a crafty Pokémon, so helping it find its way through this maze means that you have to be as crafty and cunning as well! Help Nickit work from the center out to one of four exits—but be extra careful, because only one of the exits will truly lead it out of danger, the rest lead to a Poké Ball!

CODE POKÉMON

Here's an oldie but a goodie! Hidden in the letter jumble below are recently discovered Galar Pokémon that are trying to reveal one of their lost Pokémon buddies. Color in each letter, then take the letters to unscramble the clue. We'll give you a hint—an apple a day keeps the doctor away!

POKÉMON ACROSTICS FEATURING QUAGSIRE

Let's test your creativity with Pokémon names and memory. Using Quagsire, our easy-going Pokémon, write the name in a vertical column below, then see how many LONG words you can make from each letter, but go for words that describe this particular Pokémon. We included its Pokédex entry below. For instance A = aloof! Why long words? Because you're going to be awarded one point for each letter in the word! Play against a friend or give yourself a time limit and see how creative you can get. Try it without the help of a dictionary!

Q _____

U _____

A loof   **6 POINTS** ///

G _____

S _____

I _____

R _____

E _____

It has an easygoing nature. It doesn't care if it bumps its head on boats and boulders while swimming.

PARTS NOT INCLUDED FEATURING ROOKIDEE

Rookidee is a quick one—it likes to jump about and disorient larger foes. Because of its furtive nature, it's sometimes hard to get a clear mental image of what it looks like. Let's see how quick your mental camera is—can you identify the following Pokémon and match their types by the snippets we give you below?

NORMAL

FLYING

ELECTRIC

GRASS

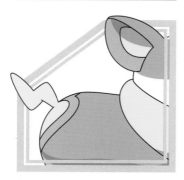

FLYING-WATER

DARK

ANSWERS ON PAGE 90 ▶

FINISH THIS POKÉMON WITH GROOKEY

Grookey is no chump—it's the Chimp Pokémon! Let's see if you remember how the colors of the rainbow apply to Grookey. Finish this line drawing of Grookey and then pick the correct color combination from the key at the bottom of the page!

Grookey has shades of which of the following colors?

1

2

3

SILICOBRA

MATCH THIS TYPE WITH SILICOBRA

Silicobra is a ground-pounder with the strength of sand behind its every move, but it does have its weaknesses. From the list of Pokémon below, match the type to the Pokémon, then identify which Pokémon would be strongest against Silicobra in a battle!

NINCADA

BUG-GROUND

GRASS

ICE

WATER

GROUND

GHOST

GLALIE

MARACTUS

DUSKNOIR

DUGTRIO

PYUKUMUKU

WHO'S THAT POKÉMON? WORD SCRAMBLE

Help us solve this Pokémon mystery. Using the Pokédex entry below, identify the missing letters, and then unscramble those letters to find our Pokémon. Time yourself for an extra challenge!

WITH ☐ VOICE LIKE A ☐UMAN CHILD'S, IT CRIES O☐T TO LURE ADULTS DEE☐ INTO THE FOREST, GETTI☐G THE☐ LOST AMONG THE ☐REES.

☐ ☐ ☐ ☐ ☐ ☐ ☐ ☐ P

CRAMORANT

POKÉMON CONNECTIONS WITH CRAMORANT

Here's a new twist. We give you a special Pokémon that we've been dying to meet—Cramorant! After we entered it into the grid, we realized there are so many other Pokémon to discover. Using our base Pokémon, see how many other Pokémon you can connect to Cramorant to make new ones! You get 50 points for each Pokémon named, and 100 points for every Pokémon you find that uses letters from at least two Pokémon on the grid! Need help? Check out the answer sheet in the back to see some of the suggestions we put into our grid. Good luck!

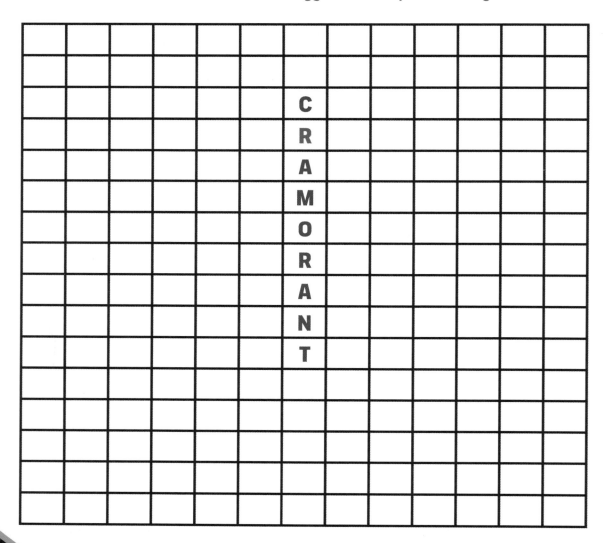

POKÉMON WALL SCRAWL WITH ELGYEM

We've got a small dilemma—during the adventure, we've come across some strange messages. They could be clues to finding some more Pokémon! Take a look at the phonetic clues below and try sounding them out to decipher the messages. You've got this!

MOOSH AR NA

DO PIH DUR

L G M

GOS IF FLEW ER

CURL LEE A

SIZE MITT ODE

ROTOM

POKÉMON SEEK AND FIND WITH ROTOM

Good job so far, Pokémon adventurer! Now we're going to test your skills at finding Pokémon in the wild, by searching through this puzzle for the Pokémon listed below. You'll notice that some Pokémon have a red letter in their name. Once you find all the Pokémon, gather up the red letters and unscramble them to find our featured Pokémon! Need a hint? It's an Electric- and Dark-type Pokémon, which is a type that is shared among the following Pokémon.

ROTOM
SABLEYE
TOGEDEMARU
RAICHU
NICKIT
MANECTRIC
UMBREON
JOLTEON
YAMPER
MANDIBUZZ
BISHARP
SCRAGGY
LIEPARD
HYDREIGON
HELIOPTILE

```
T M L C U T H R N L E I M H J H M
C S B F J F O O J V G R Y R O C A
T C M M P T G G S U W D A M L D N
R R T J M I Q S E E M T L M T R D
C A Q T E Z Z E L D S B L J E V I
B G T R Y P F I L X E A R R O Y B
K G D F D N T D M U G M B E N J U
J Y P P M P R G O A U G A L O O Z
H N D D O A L C T H N R N R E N Z
B T N I P I R S C J D E E W U Y U
V C L E Z C B I F W N P C F I R E
J E I N T U A I X K M K R T G M A
H L A I J R Y I S A N S M L R T X
X M G C K N Z Y H Z K G B J I R
X V O K B K N W C V A I V K X C C
U O E I V Q I Y K T M R R O T O M
N T P T Y E J F X C J C P C R P X
```

The Pokémon we are looking for is ___ ___ ___ ___ ___ ___ ___ ___

ANSWERS ON PAGE 91 ▶

IT TAKES ALL TYPES

Measuring your Pokémon up for battle can be tricky unless you're spot on about their type. Can you help us out? Match these types with their corresponding Pokémon, then give us any newly discovered Pokémon from the Galar region that shares at least two of those types. Let's go!

ROOKIDEE

AXEW

SYLVEON

BELLOSSOM

KLANG

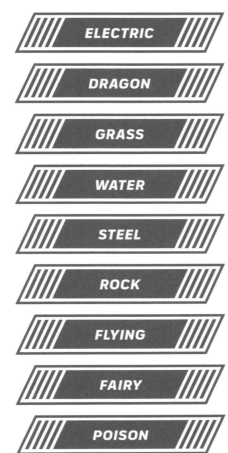

ELECTRIC

DRAGON

GRASS

WATER

STEEL

ROCK

FLYING

FAIRY

POISON

VAMPER

OCTILLERY

TRUBBISH

GIGALITH

LIST OF GALAR DUAL-TYPES THAT MATCH ONE OF THE TYPES LISTED

1. _____
2. _____
3. _____
4. _____
5. _____

6. _____
7. _____
8. _____
9. _____
10. _____

EVOLUTION ESCAPADES!

Okay, we've come about a third of the way through our journey—and now we're going back to the beginning! Let's double check your knowledge of the first Pokémon you encounter in Galar—Sobble, Grookey, and Scorbunny! Answer this true or false quiz and check your accuracy in the answer key in the back.

 **SOBBLE**

 **GROOKEY**

 **SCORBUNNY**

1. Sobble evolves into Grookey.

2. Cinderace is the final Evolution of Scorbunny.

3. Inteleon evolves into Drizzile.

4. The Evolutions of Sobble, Grookey, and Scorbunny keep a single type.

5. Raboot is taller than Thwackey.

6. Thwackey is heavier than Drizzile.

7. Thwackey is strong when fighting a Fire-type.

8. All three first partner Pokémon have a tail.

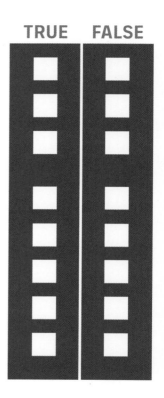

TRUE   FALSE

30

ANSWERS ON PAGE 91 ▶

POKÉMON WORD SCRAMBLE

Well, it's happened again! We lost another Pokémon, but we're sure you can help us find it. Hiding out in the Galar region, this Pokémon can be identified by its entry below. Take the missing letters and unscramble them to help us find our missing friend! Time yourself for a real challenge!

THIS ☐OKÉMON WILL ☐OOK ☐NTO ☐OUR EYES ☐ND RE☐D THE CONTE☐TS OF Y☐UR HE☐RT. IF IT FI☐DS EVIL THERE, I☐ P☐OMPTLY HIDES ☐WAY.

G	☐	☐	☐	☐	☐	☐	☐	☐

☐	☐	☐	☐	☐	☐

SHELLOS

MAZE ME WITH SHELLOS

Here's an interesting dilemma—Shellos has forms that reside on the Eastern and Western sea shores of their respective areas. But how do they get there? Help them find their way by connecting the Eastern version of each to their Western counterpart! They'll start out in their OPPOSITE areas, and you have to guide them to their correct shores. Good luck!

EXIT
TO WESTERN SEA

START

EXIT
TO EASTERN SEA

START

ANSWERS ON PAGE 91 ▶

SPOT THE DIFFERENCE WITH DREDNAW

Drednaw is a champ at chomping. But recognizing Drednaw without getting too close to its toothy maw can be a challenge. Even if you did get close, could you spot the real Drednaw from an impostor? Check out these six Drednaw pictures and see if you can spot which one is the tooth, the whole tooth, and nothing but the tooth. Time yourself for a real challenge.

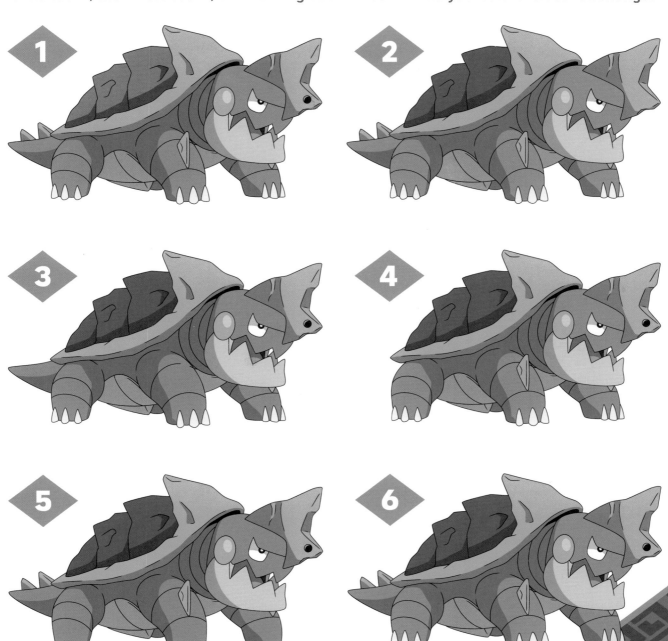

ANSWER ON PAGE 92 ▶

PARTS NOT INCLUDED WITH TRANQUIL

The Pokémon in Galar are colorful, diverse—and sometimes tricky to identify. Unlike past adventures where we try to get you to identify the Pokémon by sight, let's see if you can identify these Pokémon by part of their plumage—see what feathery friends you can identify just by their feathers!

FINISH THIS POKÉMON WITH DURALUDON

Duraludon doesn't take kindly to rain—it has to do with its sleek silver body, which rusts easily. Not many people get a glimpse of this Pokémon, but we know you can identify it easily. Finish drawing this Pokémon, then pick the color pattern that matches it and color it in—try to complete it under 30 seconds and advance to the top of the list for Pokémon adventurers!

Duraludon has shades of which of the following colors?

WHO'S THAT POKÉMON? WORD SCRAMBLE

We just can't seem to keep tabs on all the Pokémon we've met. For instance, we were looking for a certain Pokémon, whose description is below, but we still can't figure it out. Maybe if we take the missing letters and try to spell out the Pokémon, we stand a better chance? Let's hope so—help us out and see if you can figure out which Pokémon we're looking for!

□HEN FOUND THR□UGHOUT □HE GALAR REGION, THIS POKÉMON BECOME□ UNEASY IF ITS CHEE□S ARE E□ER COMPLETELY □MPTY OF BERRIES.

ANSWER ON PAGE 92 ▶

MATCH THE TYPE WITH MORPEKO

Here's a simple one that should give your weary mind a rest at this point. See if you can match the type with the dual-type Pokémon below.

MORPEKO

CORVIKNIGHT

DREDNAW

FLYING/STEEL

WATER/ROCK

MORPEKO

CRAMORANT

FLYING/WATER

GRASS/DRAGON

FLAPPLE

ELECTRIC/DARK

ANSWERS ON PAGE 92 ▶

YAMPER

ACROSTICS WITH YAMPER

Here's another test of Pokémon names! Using our example below, this time with the Puppy Pokémon, Yamper, write the name in a vertical column, then see how many LONG words you can make from each letter using words that relate to the Pokémon's Pokédex entry (included below)—for instance M=Multitude! Why long words? Because you're going to be awarded one point for each letter in the word! Play against a friend, or give yourself a time limit and see how creative you can get!

This Pokémon is very popular as a herding dog in the Galar region. As it runs, it generates electricity from the base of its tail.

Y _____

A _____

M ultitude   **9 POINTS** ////

P _____

E _____

R _____

ODD POKÉMON OUT WITH MILCERY

Help Milcery find friends of the same type by matching this type with its friends on the right. For every single-type you match, give yourself 10 points. If you find a Pokémon with a dual-type, you only get 5 points. Time yourself and play against a friend for a real challenge.

MILCERY

RIBOMBEE

SYLVEON

TOGEKISS

TOGEPI

CLEFABLE

GARDEVOIR

ANSWERS ON PAGE 92 ▶

POKÉMON CROSSWORD FEATURING LAMPENT

Ready for some more sleuthing, adventurer? Here's a simple crossword that will sharpen your skills and help you identify even more Pokémon from the Galar region.

ACROSS ////

1. Smart enough to use tools in battle, these Pokémon have been seen picking up rocks and flinging them or using ropes to wrap up enemies.

6. Its curly fleece is such an effective cushion that this Pokémon could fall off a cliff and stand right back up at the bottom, unharmed.

8. It ate a sour apple, and that induced its Evolution. In its cheeks, it stores an acid capable of causing chemical burns.

9. This Pokémon is very popular as a herding dog in the Galar region. As it runs, it generates electricity from the base of its tail.

10. A clever combatant, this Pokémon battles using water balloons created with moisture secreted from its palms.

DOWN ////

2. As it digs, it swallows sand and stores it in its neck pouch. The pouch can hold more than 17 lbs. of sand.

3. It starts off battles by attacking with its rock-hard horn, but as soon as the opponent flinches, this Pokémon bites down and never lets go.

4. By drumming, it taps into the power of its special tree stump. The roots of the stump follow its direction in battle.

5. It anchors itself in the ground with its single leg, then basks in the sun. After absorbing enough sunlight, its petals spread as it blooms brilliantly.

7. It juggles a pebble with its feet, turning it into a burning soccer ball. Its shots strike opponents hard and leave them scorched.

POKÉMON WALL SCRAWL

Oh no! We've found some more strange messages like the ones from before. Maybe these are clues to Pokémon that we lost? Could the messages be trying to tell us something? See if you can unscramble these phonetic Pokémon names and reveal their true identity. Good luck—you have 25 seconds. Shout them out loud for a better chance at deciphering them!

DO OH SHUN

VAY POOR EE AHN

L DAH GOSS

DO RAH LOO DON

CIL VAL EYE

IN TEL E AHN

FINISH THIS POKÉMON WITH RABOOT

Raboot is fast on its feet—and its thick and fluffy fur really warms it up for all its fiery moves. With all that going for it, can you remember what it looks like, and what colors it contains? Finish drawing this Pokémon and coloring in the right color combination after choosing it from the Color Key below.

Raboot has shades of which of the following colors?

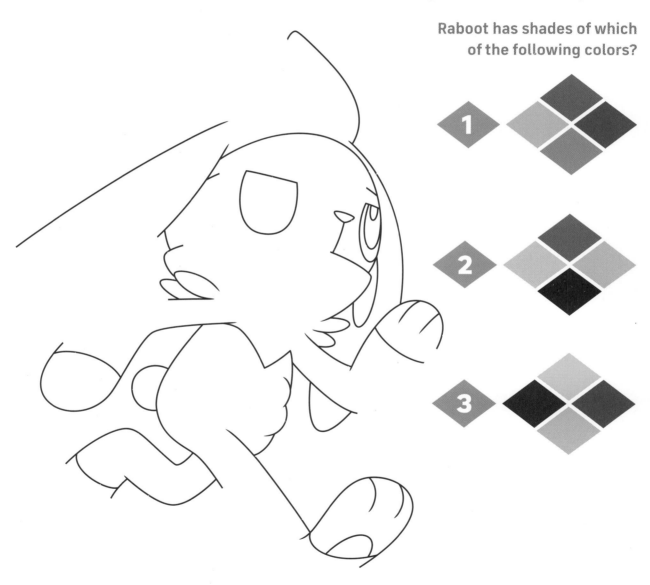

FIND THAT POKÉMON

We're really bad at keeping our Pokémon in one place! We're looking for a Galar region Pokémon, but we lost track of it—so we set up this puzzle to find that Pokémon! Solve each clue below, match it up with the picture clues on the right, and voila! The Pokémon that is found twice is the one we're looking for! Good luck!

1 Now armed with a weapon it used in ancient times, this Pokémon needs only a single strike to fell even Gigantamax Pokémon.

2 It was feared and respected by all. Though they're still only babies, there's psychic power stored in their ribbonlike feelers, and sometimes they use that power to fight.

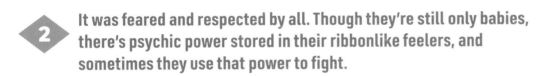

3 In the Galar region these Pokémon are brave warriors, and they wield thick, tough leeks in battle.

4 When this Pokémon is content, the cream it secretes from its hands becomes sweeter and richer.

5 The stalks of leeks are thicker and longer in the Galar region. Farfetch'd that adapted to these stalks took on a unique form.

6 Its ability to deflect any attack led to it being known as the Fighting Master's Shield.

POKÉMON NAME GAME WITH RILLABOOM

Rillaboom values consistency and harmony among its own—which is why you should definitely try your skills with this game, as it highlights your creativity and intellect. The rules for this one-player, two-player or multi-player game are simple.

RULES

FOR A ONE-PLAYER GAME:
Time yourself to see how many words you can make in a 90-second trial!

FOR TWO-PLAYER OR MULTI-PLAYER GAME:
You and a friend pick a final Evolution Pokémon like Rillaboom. Each of you writes that Pokémon's name on a piece of paper. Now come up with as many words as you can using that Pokémon's letters within a two-minute time limit. The player with the most words after two minutes wins. Good luck!

Example:
RILLABOOM
Boom
Air
Rail
Moor
Balm

POKÉMON SEEK AND FIND WITH PANGORO

PANGORO

Get ready to rumble, adventurer! There's a battle brewing in the Galar region, and the call is going out for all Trainers to report for duty.

In the Word Search below, we gave you around 20 Pokémon to find—but only 11 of them are Fighting-types. Find the Fighting-types for 50 points, but circle a non-Fighting-type, and you lose 100 points. Dual-types with Fighting as one type are acceptable. Good luck!

```
T Z K H Z T H R O H K D S Y O V N
I W W D A G V T L E X P M N Z A T
M P W E V W X C T E O D N H I N S
B W N U I X L T H I O R R M L Q K
U A X N N L Z U R A R N I A O O Q
R D C Y T P O A C P R S B Z M L B
R P E M H U C U F H S M Q F Q P D
U P P O H U R E S A A R E J Y I A
D J O R L Z O T P K C O A L X M U
S Q Y E H I T M O N C H A N E U N
N G F L F H C P A N G O R O L O K
O H W U H R P A W G A X R O Y W N
V N N L B T A C W O B T I G A B S
E Q Q L F Y A X C L U R O S L T Z
R M A C H O K E U U J M Z R Y L B
C O N K E L D U R R L A M P E N T
Y O R T I N K A Y K E K U H B M F
```

PANGORO	CONKELDURR	MACHOKE	PASSIMIAN	LUCARIO	SAWK
HAWLUCHA	FRAXURE	INKAY	CHARMELEON	DRAMPA	
TURTONATOR	HITMONCHAN	RIOLU	TIMBURR	THROH	
LAMPENT	SNOVER	ZWEILOUS	MORELULL	GOLURK	

WORD SCRAMBLE

Another day, another missing Pokémon. We should look for other work. Help us out by using the missing letters in this description to unscramble the clues. Once you get all the letters, the missing Pokémon is only a guess away.

IT COMMUNICATE☐ WITH ☐THERS TELEPATHICALLY. ITS B☐DY IS ENCAP☐ULATED IN LIQUID, BUT IF IT TAKE☐ A HEAVY BLOW, THE L☐QUID WILL ☐EAK OUT.

POKÉMON CONNECTIONS WITH CORVISQUIRE

Here's another special Pokémon that we've been wanting to meet—Corvisquire! After we entered it into the grid, we realized there are so many other Pokémon to discover. Using our base Pokémon, see how many other Pokémon you can connect to Corvisquire to make new ones! You get 50 points for each Pokémon named, and 100 points for every Pokémon you find that uses letters from at least two Pokémon on the grid! Need help? Check out the answer sheet in the back to see some of the suggestions we put into our grid. Good luck!

CORVISQUIRE

GASTRODON

MAZE ME FEATURING GASTRODON

Remember the issue we had with helping Shellos find its way back to the Eastern and Western shores? We're having the same issue with our pal Gastrodon. Help us lead Gastrodon's two forms back to their respective areas. Fastest times wins!

EXIT
TO WESTERN SEA

START

EXIT
TO EASTERN SEA

START

48

ANSWERS ON PAGE 93 ▶

SPOT THE DIFFERENCE WITH ALCREMIE

Alcremie may look like a cream puff, but it's quite formidable in battle. The problem is that all those creamy mounds look very similar. Test your visual acuity by spotting the real Alcremie amongst these imposters. Good luck—you have 20 seconds!

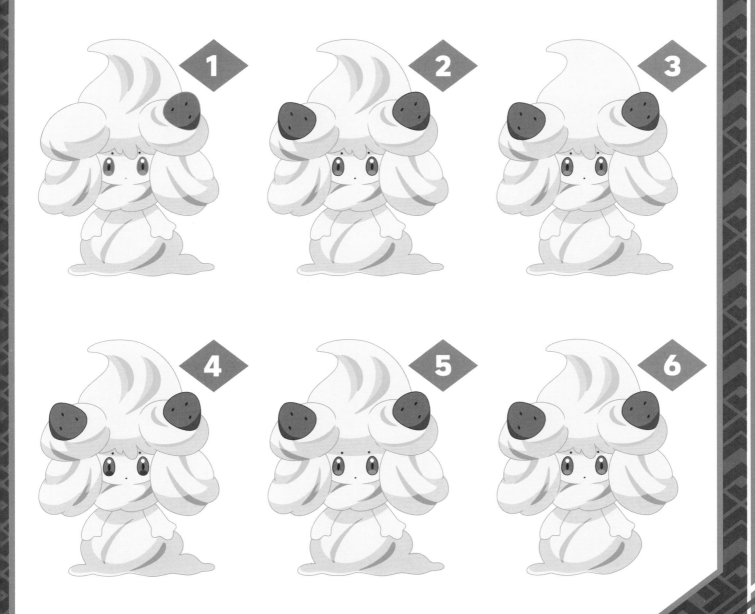

ANSWER ON PAGE 93 ▶

MATCH THE TYPE WITH DUBWOOL

Here's another test of your knowledge of Pokémon, brave adventurer! Do you know Dubwool's type? Match it with all the Pokémon on the right of the same type—but no dual types! You get 50 points for every correct answer but lose 100 if you get any wrong!

CINCCINO

BEWEAR

DUBWOOL

ORANGURU

TYPE: NULL

SKWOVET

MUNCHLAX

RUFFLET

DITTO

WORD JUMBLE FEATURING HITMONTOP

Finding this next Pokémon shouldn't be that hard—we just followed the food trail it left behind. There's another way to find it, though. Unscramble the names of these Pokémon, then enter them in order into the boxes below. Use the highlighted letter boxes to find the Pokémon that we're looking for!

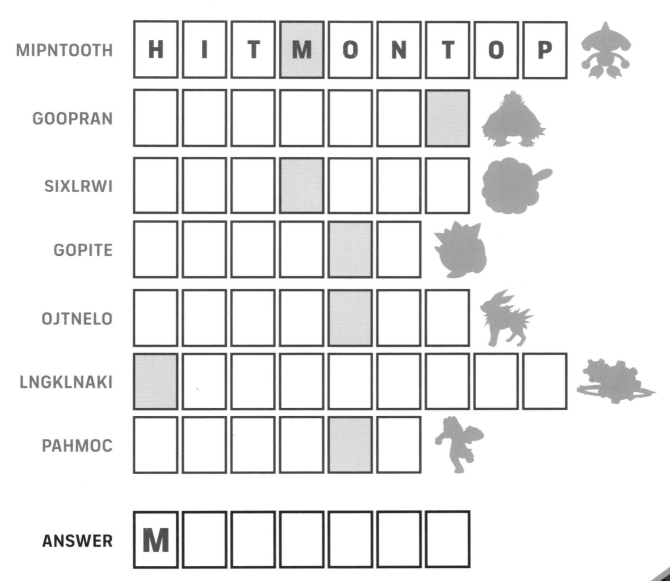

MIPNTOOTH
H I T | M O N T O P

GOOPRAN

SIXLRWI

GOPITE

OJTNELO

LNGKLNAKI

PAHMOC

ANSWER
M

NICKIT

IT TAKES ALL TYPES WITH NICKIT

Nickit is looking for similar Pokémon to hang with in Galar. Help Nickit out by identifying any Pokémon below that match Nickit's type. Dual-types are completely acceptable, so go for it!

STEENEE

MALAMAR

SABLEYE

PIKACHU

DARK-PSYCHIC

GRASS

DARK

DRAGON

ELECTRIC

DARK-GHOST

SLIGGOO

LIEPARD

YAMPER

BELLOSSOM

FINISH THIS POKÉMON WITH ZAMAZENTA

Almost there! Just help us finish this Pokémon by drawing the rest of its image, then picking the colors from the key that match. After, feel free to color in the glorious Zamazenta! Long live the Crowned Shield Pokémon!

Zamazenta is colored with shades of which of the following colors?

WALL SCRAWL WITH TOGEDEMARU

We realized that the messages we continue to find are trying to aid us in discovering more Pokémon! The cleverly hidden Pokémon names in the wall scrawl are all Pokémon we've been looking for. Let's find the last few stragglers by identifying these Pokémon from their phonetic clues. Say them out loud for an easier solution!

CARE A BLST

PA KNEE ARD

HACK SORE US

HEAL E OP TIE L

TOE GA DE MARR OOH

FER AH THORN

PARTS NOT INCLUDED
TYPE: NULL

Type: Null is one of the most unique looking Pokémon ever—so unique in fact, it's hard to tell it apart from another Pokémon. In this Parts Not Included puzzle, we give you six pieces of Pokémon below. Mark "yes" in each box below if the part belongs to Type: Null, and "no" if the part belongs to another Pokémon. Good luck!

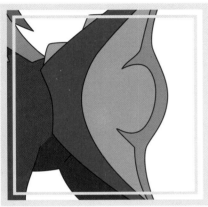

YES ☐
NO ☐

YES ☐
NO ☐

YES ☐
NO ☐

YES ☐
NO ☐

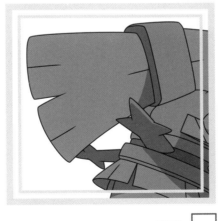

YES ☐
NO ☐

YES ☐
NO ☐

ANSWERS ON PAGE 94 ▶

GALARIAN PONYTA: RING AROUND THE COLORS

Galarian Ponyta is only one of the graceful and elegant Pokémon you'll find in Galar. But can you remember what it looked like without peeking? Identify the missing color from the drawing below, and then fill in that color yourself. You should have a picture-perfect representation of this picture-perfect Pokémon in no time!

Galarian Ponyta is missing a shade of which color?

WORD SEARCH FOR THE GROUND POUNDERS

There are a lot of Ground-type Pokémon in the Galar region. All that rich soil must be very tempting. We gave you a list of 20 Pokémon below—only nine of them are singularly Ground-types. Choose carefully, because for every Ground-type you get 50 points, but circle a non-Ground-type, and you lose 100 points. You can do this!

```
M U D B R A Y Q V S A V A L U G G
Q H M U L F K V P A V B H F D U V
V I J P S R D V K Y N O Z W U T F
T P V E D E S O L O S I S L G J I
D P B R P Q D M A G F Y L O T A Z
I O K S H P Q I X D L F T L R E N
G P H I P P O W D O N T I I I S Y
L O L A Y O P M E M I T J N O T G
E T S N G T T A Y D U X X J G E E
T A N C I T R R F X Y D T V W E R
T S E J E Z K A S R V J S X L N N
L U N E H Q O C P P O Q J D E E U
K S M O O B D T A I M S Z N A E Z
N F U T N G Z U M A N D L L L S L L
C I V L N R P S A W X C L A Q P E
S I L I C O B R A T K Q H O S I A
L D R I L B U R M E R P W H Z S F
```

HIPPOWDON

DIGLETT

DIGLETT	DITTO	MUDBRAY	VANILLITE
STEENEE	DRILBUR	NUZLEAF	DUGTRIO
HIPPOPOTAS	KOFFING	TRAPINCH	FROSLASS
PERSIAN	MUDSDALE	MARACTUS	AVALUGG
SILICOBRA	SOLOSIS	HIPPOWDON	SILICOBRA

SPOT THE DIFFERENCE WITH THWACKEY

Thwackey likes to "drum up" trouble, but it dances to its own beat. With all that vibration going on, you might have some trouble keeping a steady eye on Thwackey. Let's test that. Below are six different images of Thwackey—but only one is the real deal. See if you can spot the true Thwackey, but try to keep it under 60 seconds if possible, then test a friend and see how long it takes them. Good luck!

HOW MANY CAN YOU NAME?

Using your knowledge of the newly discovered Galar Pokémon (you can use our handy-dandy chart in the back of the book for reference), see how many of these questions you can answer within a two-minute time limit. Ready, set, go!

1 How many newly discovered Galar Pokémon have Fairy-types in at least one of their types? _____

2 How many newly discovered Galar Pokémon only have one type? _____
_____
_____

3 How many newly discovered Galar Pokémon are Electric-type or dual-type with electric in it? _____

4 How many newly discovered Galar Pokémon can fly or float? _____
_____

5 How many newly discovered Galar Pokémon have antennae? _____

6 How many newly discovered Galar Pokémon are 1" or smaller? _____
_____

7 How many newly discovered Galar Pokémon have dual forms? _____
_____

8 How many newly discovered Galar Pokémon have a W in their name? _____
_____

9 How many newly discovered Galar Pokémon are quadruped (walk on all fours)?
_____

WHO'S THAT POKÉMON? FEATURING INTELEON

Inteleon uses water as a weapon—shooting water from its fingertips at up to Mach 3! That's some jet stream! But quick on the draw doesn't mean Inteleon always hits the right target. Help Inteleon choose the correct Pokémon rival by identifying these six Pokémon from their silhouettes. Try to do so in 90 seconds or fewer, or you may be drinking salt water for breakfast!

1

_____

2
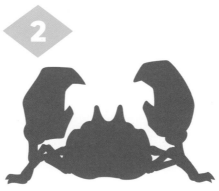
_____

3

_____

4

_____

5

_____

6

_____

ANSWERS ON PAGE 94 ▶

CODE POKÉMON

Okay, we've lost enough Pokémon for the day! Help us out by solving this puzzle. Check the Pokémon at the bottom of the page, then color in their letter in the jumble below. Once you have all those letters filled in, match the letter to the Pokémon, and you'll spell out the missing Pokémon! Stay in the lines, adventurer!

CRYPTOGLYPHICS

Again, with the missing Pokémon? We should really hire more people. Using the entry below, fill in the blanks with the letters represented by each Pokémon, and you should find our missing Pokémon in short time.

LEGEND

L	M	B	R	A	I

BY D[R]UMM[I]NG, [I]T T[A]PS [I]NTO THE POWE[R] OF [I]TS SPEC[I][A][L] T[R]EE STUMP. THE [R]OOTS OF THE STUMP FO[L][L]OW [I]TS D[I][R]ECTION [I]N [B]A[A]TT[L]E. [I]T'S N[A]ME IS [R][I][L][L][A][B]OO[M].

POKÉMON CHECKLIST

We are finally rounding up all of our missing Pokémon. One seems to have slipped through, though, and we're sure it's around here somewhere. Here's a series of clues. How many do you need to solve the mystery? If you can solve this head-scratcher in four clues or less, give yourself a bonus 100 points!

1 It's a clever combatant, this Pokémon battles using water balloons created with moisture secreted from its palms.

2 It evolves from this Pokémon

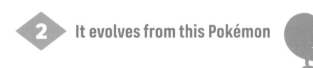

3 It is highly intelligent but also very lazy, and it keeps enemies out of its territory by laying traps everywhere.

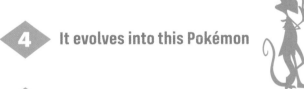

4 It evolves into this Pokémon

5 It's a single type—Water-type.

6 It weighs 25.4 lbs. and is 2'04" tall.

7 It is known as the Water Lizard Pokémon.

This Pokémon is

_____ _____ _____ _____ _____ _____ _____ _____ _____

ANSWER ON PAGE 95 ▶

POKÉMON NAME GAME FEATURING CHANDELURE

Here's a little distraction to ease you out of all the Pokémon training you've been doing so far. We picked Chandelure, that dancing, prancing ghostly Pokémon as your example—write its name on a piece of paper (separate pieces of paper if you're playing with a friend,) then race to see how many words you can think of within a two-minute time limit. The player with the most words after two minutes wins. Good luck!

RULES

FOR A ONE-PLAYER GAME:
Time yourself to see how many words you can make in a 90-second trial!

FOR TWO-PLAYER OR MULTI-PLAYER GAME:
You and a friend pick a final Evolution Pokémon like Rillaboom. Each of you writes that Pokémon's name on a piece of paper. Now come up with as many words as you can using that Pokémon's letters within a two-minute time limit. The player with the most words after two minutes wins. Good luck!

Example:
CHANDELURE
Head
Lead
Land
Hand
Candle

NEVER-ENDING ESCAPADES WITH GALARIAN FARFETCH'D

It's a sight to see Farfetch'd in Galar—we've seen it before, but never in its Galarian form. We wonder if you know enough about this Pokémon to help us find it and catch it. Answer these true or false questions, and give yourself 25 points for each right answer, but subtract 50 points for each one you miss! Good luck!

	TRUE	FALSE
1. Galarian Farfetch'd carries a bamboo stick in its mouth.	☐	☐
2. It weighs under 100 lbs.	☐	☐
3. Galarian Farfetch'd is a Flying-type Pokémon.	☐	☐
4. When it comes to feathers, Galarian Farfetch'd has brightly colored blue feathers.	☐	☐
5. The beak and feet of Galarian Farfetch'd is the same color.	☐	☐
6. It is known as the Wild Duck Pokémon.	☐	☐
7. The stalk of the plant it carries is thicker and stronger in the Galar region.	☐	☐
8. Galarian Farfetch'd are known to be cowardly and sneaky.	☐	☐
9. Galarian Farfetch'd is a Fighting- and Psychic-type Pokémon.	☐	☐
10. In a battle, Galarian Farfetch'd would be strong against Fairy- and Psychic-type Pokémon.	☐	☐

GALARIAN FARFETCH'D

ANSWERS ON PAGE 95 ▶

HOOTHOOT

MATCH THE TYPE WITH HOOTHOOT

Hoothoot is a Pokémon that knows its strength and weaknesses—it's also a dual-type Pokémon. Let's see if you know other Pokémon that are dual-type. Match the Pokémon below to the dual-types in the middle and we'll trust you to find the remaining Pokémon for us! We need the help!

CHARIZARD

GOURGEIST

GLOOM

GRASS-POISON

GHOST-GRASS

FIRE-FLYING

ICE-GROUND

DRAGON-NORMAL

GHOST-FAIRY

SWINUB

MIMIKYU

DRAMPA

ODD POKÉMON OUT FEATURING PICHU

Almost there, adventurer! Help us round up the remaining Pokémon by identifying the Pichu we have on our team with other Electric-type Pokémon in the area. Below are Pokémon that are Electric-type. Only choose the ones that are pure Electric-type only. Good luck!

PICHU

ELECTRIKE

TOGEDEMARU

HELIOLISK

JOLTEON

CHINCHOU

YAMPER

ROTOM

CHARJABUG

MORPEKO

POKÉMON ACROSTICS WITH FLYGON

Let's test your creativity with Pokémon names and memory. Using Flygon, our sandstorm-hiding friend, write the name in a vertical column, then see how many LONG words you can make from each letter, but go for words that describe this particular Pokémon. We included its Pokédex entry below—for instance L = lenticular! Why long words? Because you're going to be awarded one point for each letter in the word! Play against a friend or give yourself a time limit and see how creative you can get—no cheating! Put that dictionary away!

F _____

L _enticular_   `10 POINTS ////` _____

Y _____

G _____

O _____

N _____

This Pokémon hides in the heart of sandstorms it creates and seldom appears where people can see it.

SPOT THE DIFFERENCE WITH GLOOM

We encountered Gloom along the way while adventuring through the Galar region—but we found several—and we think that only one of them might be the real deal! Help us out here—take a good look at the following images and tell us which Gloom is the right one. Do it in under 30 seconds and we're on the way to finishing up our mission here in the Galar region.

ANSWER ON PAGE 95 ▶

CRYPTOGLYPHICS

We have another runner! A Pokémon has slipped through our grasp once again, but we are so close to finding it. Help! Decipher the clues below and use the cryptographic to solve this puzzle.

LEGEND

I H N O T M P

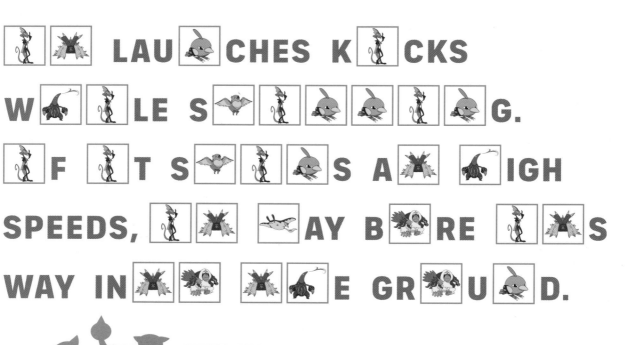

IT LAUNCHES KICKS WHILE SPINNING. IF IT SPINS AT HIGH SPEEDS, IT MAY BORE ITS WAY INTO THE GROUND.

ANSWER ON PAGE 95 ▶

CHERRIM WORD SEARCH

You'll find many Grass-type Pokémon in Galar, especially in the tall grass areas. We found a Cherrim, but we're on the search for all of its Grass-type buddies as well. In the following word search, there are 20 Pokémon listed, but only 10 of them are pure Grass-types. Give yourself a good two minutes to carefully pick out the Grass-type Pokémon from the list. You get 25 points for each correct find, but deduct 50 points if you pick any dual types with Grass-type in it. Go!

CHERRIM

```
D N H T Q G O S S I F L E U R D E
Z G Q R L U E U W S N G W N V S R
W R K N Z I T T S A R E E N A W P
P Z O U S C Q B A R D I L S Z H V
J K E S A A X B O U T V U T F I G
K I W R E Q E B B U E J G E P M F
W L A X M R M Q J J N J Y E N S B
S M E T H W A C K E Y S D N J I C
H F H A G K O D S T F W W E U C E
I Y A I F X S R E N Q S E E D O T
F C A A L E N F L A P P L E E T H
T H F G R O O K E Y H C W D A T O
R E O C V H V N F E R R O S E E D
Y R P R I P E W A T I K Q B M T D
C R X F Q G R A B O M A S N O W I
J I Q C Z Z P Z A N Z S X M W C B S
O M O R E L U L L Q M O X C Z W H
```

CHERRIM
WHIMSICOTT
SEEDOT
ABOMASNOW
GROOKEY
ROSERADE
LEAFEON
FERROSEED
STEENEE
BUDEW
MARACTUS
MORELULL
TSAREENA
FLAPPLE
GOSSIFLEUR
SHIFTRY
THWACKEY
ODDISH
BOUNSWEET
SNOVER

ANSWERS ON PAGE 95 ▶

WHO'S THAT POKÉMON? FEATURING SNOVER

We're almost there. Our Snover, which is an icy little fighter, is helping us round up the remaining Pokémon in the Galar region. See if you can find these Pokémon just by looking at their silhouettes. That would be an awesome help to us! Oh, and these Pokémon would be weak in battle against Snover!

1

2

3

4

5

6

WALL SCRAWL WITH OCTILLERY

We got in contact with the ones responsible for scrawling these Pokémon names everywhere! Seems they really want us to find every Pokémon out there, and they've been leaving hints as to which ones we've missed. Decipher these phonetic clues to find some of the Pokémon we're missing.

GA THO REE TA

DUSS KLOPSE

AWK TILL EERIE

CHREV IN IN T

SHIE KNOT ICKE

WIM SIK OTT

ROGGENROLA

MATCH THIS TYPE WITH ROGGENROLA

Roggenrola is a tough Pokémon to crack. It gets so powerful that the energy core inside it makes Roggenrola slightly warm to the touch. But it isn't unbeatable. From the list of Pokémon below, match the type to the Pokémon, then identify which Pokémon would be strongest against Roggenrolla in a normal battle!

ACCELGOR

DIGLETT

STEENEE

ARCANINE

GLALIE

GURDURR

VAPOREON

ELECTRIKE

KLANG

GRASS

FIGHTING

STEEL

ELECTRIC

FIRE

WATER

BUG

GROUND

ICE

RING AROUND THE COLORS WITH RIBOMBEE

Beautiful Pokémon fill the Galar region, such as the graceful and delicate Ribombee. We'll give you three color shade choices, and without looking it up in the back of the book, see if you can color Ribombee in with the correct combination!

Ribombee uses shades of which colors?

1

2

3

WORD SCRAMBLE

Help us find another missing Pokémon! Using the Pokédex entry below, identify the missing letters, and then unscramble those letters to find our Pokémon. Time yourself for an extra challenge!

A ☐OUGH ☐☐STOMER TH☐T WIL☐LY FLAILS ITS GIA☐T CLA☐S. IT IS SAID TO BE EXTREMELY H☐RD ☐O RAISE.

☐ ☐ ☐ ☐ ☐ ☐ ☐ ☐ ☐

ANSWERS ON PAGE 96 ▶

MAZE ME: PIDOVE TO TRANQUILL TO UNFEZANT

We lost a whole Evolution chain of Pokémon! But we have a chance to get them back. Start with Pidove, work your way to Tranquill, then meet Unfezant at the exit. If you see any other stray Pokémon along the way, let us know!

CODE POKÉMON

Okay, even we know we have to clean this mess up. Help us with the last few Pokémon—we're almost there! Color in the letters outlined in the Pokémon list below to uncover one of the remaining Pokémon we're after. Use the key to find your letters.

ANSWER ON PAGE 96 ▶

PARTS NOT INCLUDED FEATURING KLINKLANG

We are almost home—we only have a few Pokémon to round up! One of them is our friend Klinklang, who we keep an eye on, because when that core starts glowing red, it means the energy it stores is ready to be released. Problem is, we saw a few Klinklang—or maybe just a few fakes. Help us find the real Klinklang!

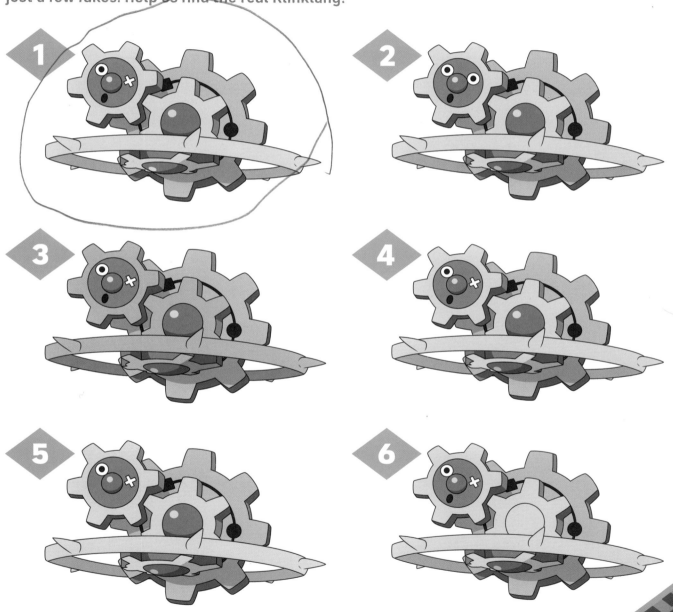

GALVANTULA

SEEK AND FIND WITH GALVANTULA

How about a tiny break before we get to the final Pokémon?
Help us find the following Pokémon in the grid below, which
Galvantula was very helpful in rounding up. But Galvantula knows what
its type is strong and weak against, so it's looking for Pokémon that are also the same
type. In the list of 20 Pokémon below, find the other Bug- and Electric-type Pokémon.
We're desperate! Find all Bug- and Electric-types, regardless of if they're single or dual.

MUDBRAY 	NOCTOWL 	VIKAVOLT 	TYRANITAR 	JOLTEON 
GRUBBIN 	BERGMITE 	PIKACHU 	MANECTRIC 	SKWOVET 
GASTLY 	CATERPIE 	JOLTIK 	SALAZZLE 	GOTHITELLE 
SHELMET 	MAWILE 	METAPOD 	SILICOBRA 	CHARJABUG 

ANSWERS ON PAGE 96 ▶

ODD POKÉMON OUT FEATURING SOLOSIS

Solosis is one of our few remaining Pokémon—but it won't come with us unless we find other Pokémon that share its type. Pick two Pokémon from below that match its type—but match it exactly! It communicates with others telepathically, so be careful!

SOLOSIS

WOBBUFFET

XATU

SWOOBAT

RALTS

GARDEVOIR

MIME JR.

MUNNA

SIGILYPH

ANSWERS ON PAGE 96 ▶

EVOLUTION ESCAPADES!

We have a chance to find a whole missing Evolution chain at once—and we're going to take it. But first you're going to have to answer some true or false questions before they're released to us! Answer this true or false quiz and check your accuracy in the answer key in the back.

GOTHITA

GOTHORITA

GOTHITELLE

TRUE FALSE

1. Gothita is the middle Evolution of its chain.

2. The color blue shows up in their appearance

3. All three Pokémon are dual-types.

4. All three Pokémon are Psychic-types.

5. None of them is over 5'00" tall.

6. You can clearly see the legs of each Pokémon in this chain.

7. Though they're still only babies, Gothita's psychic power is stored in their ribbonlike feelers, and sometimes they use that power to fight.

8. At least one in this Evolution chain is over 100 lbs.

9. Their eyes are a psychic, mysterious green.

10. Gothita is known as the Fixation Pokémon.

POKÉMON NAME GAME WITH REUNICLUS

We can feel the end of our journey coming. Help us out by playing this fun game that will test your creativity and help us gather up Reuniclus!

RULES

You and a friend pick a final evolution Pokémon like Reuniclus. Each of you writes that Pokémon name on a piece of paper. Now, come up with as many words as you can using that Pokémon's letters within a two-minute time limit. The player with the most words after two minutes wins. Good luck!

Example:

REUNICLUS
Rune
User
Cure
Slur

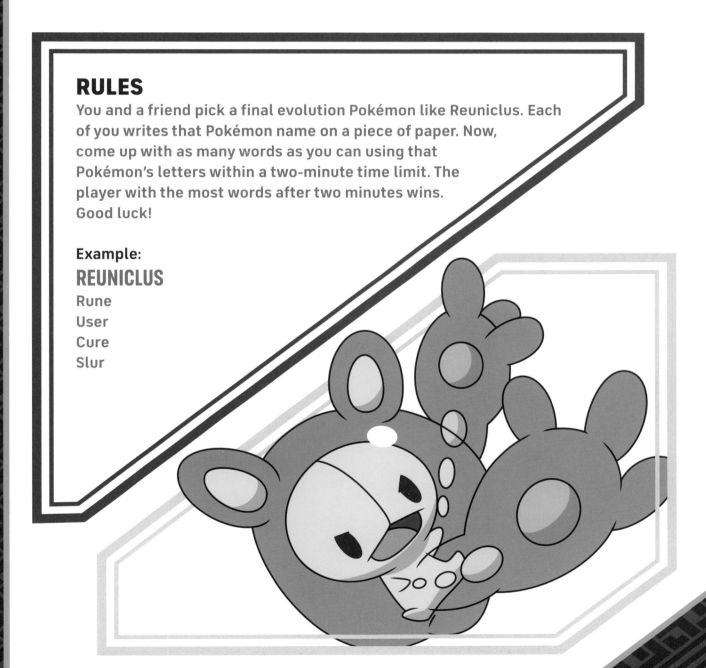

WALL SCRAWL WITH SNEASEL

It must be our lucky day! Thanks to all the messages we've been finding on our adventure, we haven't been falling behind on discovering as many Pokémon as we can! Here's the last set of scrawls we found—help us decipher them by shouting them out loud!

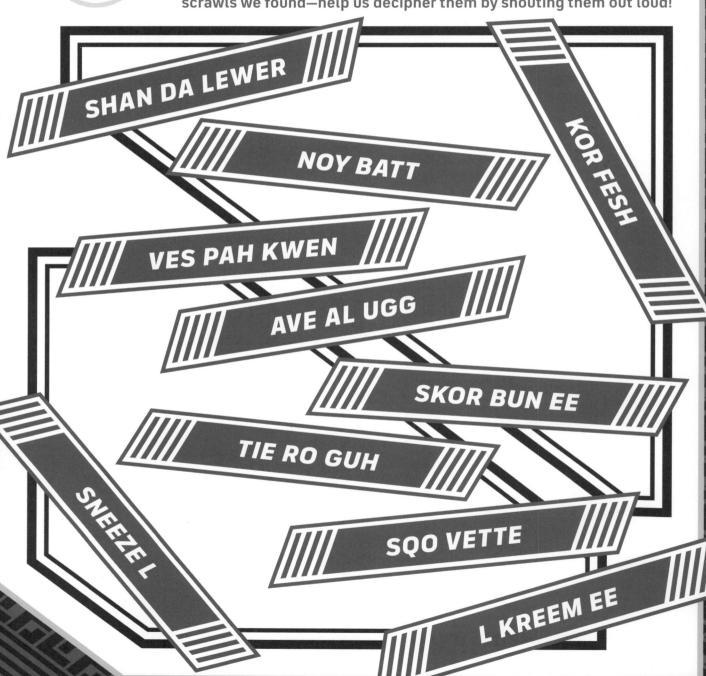

SHAN DA LEWER

NOY BATT

KOR FESH

VES PAH KWEN

AVE AL UGG

SKOR BUN EE

TIE RO GUH

SNEEZE L

SQO VETTE

L KREEM EE

ETERNATUS WORD CONNECTION

You know we're finishing things up when you see us hitting the Legendary Pokémon! We give you a special Pokémon that we've been waiting to meet—Eternatus! After we entered it into the grid, we realized there are so many other Pokémon to discover. Using our base Pokémon, see how many other Pokémon you can connect to Eternatus to make new ones! You get 50 points for each Pokémon named, and 100 points for every Pokémon you find that uses letters from at least two Pokémon on the grid! Need help? Check out the answer sheet in the back to see some of the suggestions we put into our grid. Good luck!

						E							
						T							
						E							
						R							
						N							
						A							
						T							
						U							
						S							

ANSWERS ON PAGE 96 ▶

TOGEKISS

EVOLUTION CROSSWORD

Here's a different challenge! This crossword puzzle is made up of just evolved Pokémon. See how many of these Pokémon you can identify by their description, and we'll even throw a hint by giving you which Pokémon they evolved from or into. Good luck—we'll give you an extra two minutes for this tough puzzle!

ACROSS

1. It makes pollen puffs from pollen and nectar. The puffs' effects depend on the type of ingredients and how much of each one is used. Evolved from Cutiefly.

3. It launches electrified fur from its abdomen as its means of attack. Opponents hit by the fur could be in for three full days and nights of paralysis. Evolved from Joltik.

5. It kicks berries right off the branches of trees and then juggles them with its feet, practicing its footwork. Evolves from Scorbunny and into Cinderace.

7. It has many hidden capabilities, such as fingertips that can shoot water and a membrane on its back that it can use to glide through the air. Evolves from Drizzile.

8. When it's drumming out rapid beats in battle, it gets so caught up in the rhythm that it won't even notice that it's already knocked out its opponent. Evolves from Grookey and into Rillaboom.

9. Highly intelligent but also very lazy, it keeps enemies out of its territory by laying traps everywhere. Evolves from Sobble and into Inteleon.

DOWN

1. By drumming, it taps into the power of its special tree stump. The roots of the stump follow its direction in battle. Evolves from Thwackey.

2. It juggles a pebble with its feet, turning it into a burning soccer ball. Its shots strike opponents hard and leave them scorched. Evolves from Raboot.

4. This Pokémon is intelligent and intensely proud. People will sit up and take notice if you become the Trainer of one. Evolves from Tranquil.

6. These Pokémon are never seen anywhere near conflict or turmoil. In recent times, they've hardly been seen at all. Evolves from Togetic.

CINDERACE

WHO'S THAT POKÉMON? WORD SCRAMBLE

Welcome to the final stop in your journey to help us find all the Pokémon we could in the Galar region. It's been a wild ride, but a whole lot of fun. We have one Pokémon not on our list. If you can guess who it is, we can all go home! Use the missing letters from the clue below and then unscramble those letters to find this Legendary Pokémon that we need to complete our adventure! You've been great, so we're going to start you off with the first letter. Good luck!

⬜BLE TO CUT DOWN ANYTHING WITH A SINGLE STRIKE, IT BE⬜AME KNOWN AS THE FAIRY KI⬜G'S SWORD, AND IT INSPIRED ⬜WE IN FRIEND AND FOE AL⬜KE.

Z	⬜	⬜	⬜	⬜	⬜

88

ANSWERS ON PAGE 96 ▶

ANSWER KEY

PAGE 6

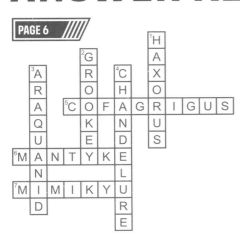

Crossword answers:
- H: HAXORUS
- G: GROOKEY
- A: ARAQUANID
- C: CHANDELURE
- COFAGRIGUS
- MANTYKE
- MIMIKYU

PAGE 7

LUNATONE: ROCK-PSYCHIC

PURRLOIN: DARK

KINGLER: WATER

GOODRA: DRAGON

MANECTRIC: ELECTRIC

PICHU: ELECTRIC

PAGE 8

KARRABLAST
PIKACHU
RILLABOOM
CHINCHOU
GOLISOPOD
MILOTIC
Answer: RABOOT

PAGE 9

1. MEOWSTIC
2. GARBODOR
3. QUAGSIRE
4. SHUCKLE
5. SCORBUNNY
6. SUDOWOODO
7. SYLVEON

PAGE 10

1. 22
2. 10
3. 15
4. 6
5. 20
6. 6
7. GRASS

PAGE 11

1 [corviknight image]

PAGE 12

SKWOVET
EEVEE
BUNNELBY
GREEDENT
SNORLAX

PAGE 13

WITH JAWS THAT CAN SHEAR THROUGH STEEL RODS, THIS HIGHLY AGGRESSIVE POKÉMON CHOMPS DOWN ON ITS UNFORTUNATE PREY.

DREDNAW

PAGE 14

```
K Z K I S G A S T R O D O N P J O
T Y Y K J N C H E W T L E K I J M
L D O G R O O K E Y V Z I A D S P
J P J T X X U V A W T F M J O H J
X G A P P W H W E Z K H A U B E M R
N I C K I T A O O R O W H B E A S
P Y J R P N I N Z S Y L I X E A T
A I V D D I N I U N S H L W R J J
Y N Q E A D Q X N O C G E P L R H
A V R J L S B U B R B B A S A J W
B D T F G A B A U V L K A S W A C
L A N U U R O A O N M I L O T I U
B O L D O R E V I T W H E N B J K
A X X C V I L E P L U M E N Q R E
L I S A E N Z Q W M D Z I W G J Y
M U D S D A L E G A I H A C J I P
N X B Q R U F R E D O S O B B L E
```

The Pokémon we are looking for is ETERNATUS.

PAGE 15

RHYDON   BISHARP   SILVALLY   AXEW   ESCAVALIER   TYRANITAR

PAGE 16

1. STEELIX   2. SNORLAX   3. AVALUGG   4. ZAMAZENTA   5. MUDSDALE   6. ETERNATUS

PAGE 17

PAGE 18

PAGE 19

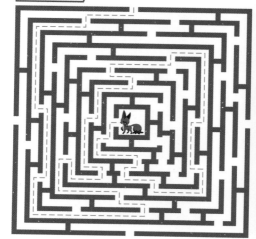

PAGE 20

FLAPPLE

Answer: FLAPPLE

PAGE 22

ROOKIDEE: FLYING   SKWOVET: NORMAL   YAMPER: ELECTRIC   RILLABOOM: GRASS   CRAMORANT: FLYING-WATER   NICKIT: DARK

PAGE 23

PAGE 24

NINCADA: BUG-GROUND   MARACTUS: GRASS   DUGTRIO: GROUND   GLALIE: ICE   DUSKNOIR: GHOST   PYUKUMUKU: WATER

PAGE 25

WITH A VOICE LIKE A HUMAN CHILD'S, IT CRIES OUT TO LURE ADULTS DEEP INTO THE FOREST, GETTING THEM LOST AMONG THE TREES.

PHANTUMP

PAGE 26

EXAMPLE:

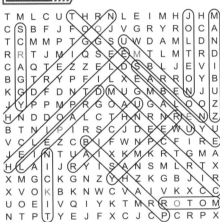

PAGE 27

MOOSH AR NA:	MUSHARNA
DO PIE DUR:	DEWPIDER
L G M:	ELGYEM
GOS IF FLEW ER:	GOSSIFLEUR
CURL LEE A:	KIRLIA
SIZE MITT ODE:	SEISMITOAD

PAGE 28

[word search grid]

The Pokémon we are looking for is MORPEKO.

PAGE 30

1. FALSE	5. FALSE
2. TRUE	6. TRUE
3. FALSE	7. FALSE
4. TRUE	8. TRUE

PAGE 31

THIS POKÉMON WILL LOOK INTO YOUR EYES AND READ THE CONTENTS OF YOUR HEART. IF IT FINDS EVIL THERE, IT PROMPTLY HIDES AWAY.

The Pokémon we seek is GALARIAN PONYTA

PAGE 29

AXEW: DRAGON

SYLVEON: FAIRY

BELLOSSOM: GRASS

KLANG: STEEL

ROOKIDEE: FLYING

YAMPER: ELECTRIC

OCTILLERY: WATER

TRUBBISH: POISON

GIGALITH: ROCK

1. FLAPPLE: GRASS-DRAGON
2. ZACIAN: FAIRY-STEEL
3. GLOOM: GRASS-POISON
4. CORVIKNIGHT: FLYING-STEEL
5. NINETALES: FIRE
6. MORPEKO: ELECTRIC-DARK
7. CRAMORANT: WATER-FLYING
8. ETERNATUS: POISON-DRAGON
9. DREDNAW: WATER-ROCK
10. DURALUDON: STEEL-DRAGON

PAGE 32

PAGE 33

6

PAGE 34

1. GALARIAN FARFETCH'D 2. CORVIKNIGHT 3. CRAMORANT

4. CORVISQUIRE 5. ROOKIDEE 6. TRANQUIL

PAGE 35

1

PAGE 36

WHEN FOUND THROUGHOUT THE GALAR REGION, THIS POKÉMON BECOMES UNEASY IF ITS CHEEKS ARE EVER COMPLETELY EMPTY OF BERRIES.

SKWOVET

PAGE 37

CORVIKNIGHT: FLYING-STEEL

DREDNAW: WATER-ROCK

MORPEKO: ELECTRIC-DARK

CRAMORANT: FLYING-WATER

FLAPPLE: GRASS-DRAGON

PAGE 39

RIBOMBEE: FAIRY-BUG

SYLVEON: FAIRY

TOGEKISS: FAIRY-FLYING

GARDEVOIR: FAIRY-PSYCHIC

CLEFABLE: FAIRY

TOGEPI: FAIRY

PAGE 40

Crossword:
1 (across): CORVISQUIRE
6 (across): WOOLOO
8 (across): FLAPPLE
9 (across): YAMPER
10 (across): DRIZZILE
Down: CHEWTLE, SILICOBRA, RILLABOO, GOSSIFLEUR, CINDERACE

PAGE 41

VAY POOR EE AHN: VAPOREON
L DAH GOSS: ELDEGOSS
CIL VAL EE: SILVALLY
IN TEL E AHN: INTELEON
DO OH SHUN: DUOSION
DO RAH LOO DON: DURALUDON

PAGE 42

2

PAGE 43

1. ZACIAN 2. GOTHITA 3. GALARIAN FARFETCH'D

4. ALCREMIE 5. GALARIAN FARFETCH'D 6. ZAMAZENTA

PAGE 45

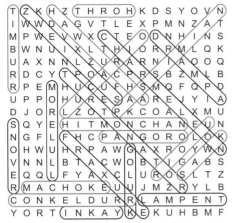

Answers circled in red are Fighting-types.

PAGE 46

IT COMMUNICATES WITH OTHERS TELEPATHICALLY. ITS BODY IS ENCAPSULATED IN LIQUID, BUT IF IT TAKES A HEAVY BLOW, THE LIQUID WILL LEAK OUT.

SOLOSIS

PAGE 47

EXAMPLE:

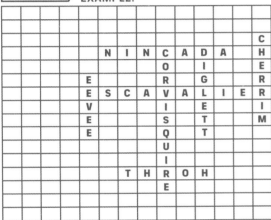

PAGE 48

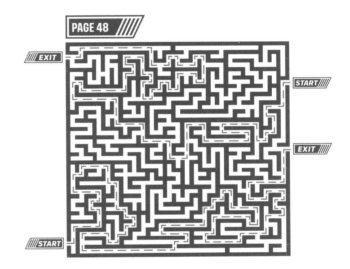

PAGE 49

PAGE 50

These Pokémon are all normal types.

CINCCINO   MUNCHLAX   SKWOVET   TYPE: NULL   DITTO

PAGE 51

PANGORO
SWIRLIX
TOGEPI
JOLTEON
KLINKLANG
MACHOP
Answer: MORPEKO

PAGE 52

STEENEE: GRASS

MALAMAR: DARK-PSYCHIC

SABLEYE: DARK-GHOST

PIKACHU: ELECTRIC

SLIGGOO: DRAGON

LIEPARD: DARK

YAMPER: ELECTRIC

BELLOSSOM: GRASS

PAGE 53

PAGE 54

CARE A BLST: KARRABLAST
PA KNEE ARD: PAWNIARD
HACK SORE US: HAXORUS
HEAL E OP TIE L: HELIOPTILE
TOE GA DE MARR OOH: TOGEDEMARU
FER AH THORN: FERROTHORN

PAGE 55

TYPE:NULL: YES   ROGGENROLA: NO   ROTOM: NO

UMBREON: NO   TYPE:NULL: YES   TYPE:NULL: YES

PAGE 56

PAGE 57

```
M U D B R A Y Q V S A V A L U G G
Q H M U L F K V P A V B H F D U V
V I J P S R D V K Y N O Z W U T F
T P V E D E S O L O S I S L G J A
D I P B K P Q D M A G F Y L O T I Z
I O L O P S H P Q I X D L F T R E N
G T L A Y O P M E M I J N O T S Y
L E A N G T T A Y D U X X J G E G
E J E Z K A S R V J S X L E N E R
L U N E H Q O C P P O O J D E E N
K S M O O B D T A I M S Z N A E U
N F U T N G Z U M A N D L L S L Z
C I V L N R P S A W X C L A Q P E
S I L I C O B R A T K Q H O S I A F
L D R I L B U R M E R P W H Z S
```

PAGE 58

3

PAGE 59

1. THREE: Milcery, Alcremie, Zacian
2. TWENTY-FIVE: Nickit, Yamper, Milcery, Alcremie, Raboot, Cinderace, Scorbunny, Corvisquire, Rookidee, Grookey, Rillaboom, Thwackey, Gossifleur, Eldegoss, Silicobra, Greedent, Wooloo, Skwovet, Dubwool, Galarian Ponyta, Chewtle, Drizzile, Sobble, Inteleon
3. TWO: Yamper, Morpeko
4. EIGHT: Eternatus, Eldegoss, Gossifleur, Rookidee, Cramorant, Corvisquire, Corviknight, Milcery
5. ZERO
6. ELEVEN: Yamper, Morpeko, Milcery, Alcremie, Scorbunny, Rookidee, Grookey, Flapple, Chewtle, Skwovet, Sobble
7. FOUR: Morpeko, Alcremie, Zacian, Zamazenta,
8. SIX: Thwackey, Wooloo, Skwovet, Dubwool, Chewtle, Drednaw
9. ELEVEN: Drednaw, Sobble, Chewtle, Galarian Ponyta, Dubwool, Wooloo, Zamazenta, Zacian, Yamper, Nickit

PAGE 60

TYPE: NULL   KRABBY   SOLROCK   BRONZONG

AEGISLASH   XATU

PAGE 61

Answer: CINDERACE

94

PAGE 62

BY DRUMMING, IT TAPS INTO THE POWER OF ITS SPECIAL TREE STUMP. THE ROOTS OF THE STUMP FOLLOW ITS DIRECTION IN BATTLE. ITS NAME IS RILLABOOM.

PAGE 63

DRIZZILE

PAGE 65

1. FALSE
2. TRUE
3. FALSE
4. FALSE
5. TRUE
6. TRUE
7. TRUE
8. FALSE
9. FALSE
10. FALSE

PAGE 66

CHARIZARD: FIRE-FLYING

GOURGEIST: GHOST-GRASS

GLOOM: GRASS-POISON

SWINUB: ICE-GROUND

MIMIKYU: GHOST-FAIRY

DRAMPA: DRAGON-NORMAL

PAGE 67

ELECTRIKE

JOLTEON

YAMPER

PAGE 69

PAGE 70

IT LAUNCHES KICKS WHILE SPINNING. IF IT SPINS AT HIGH SPEED, IT MAY BORE ITS WAY INTO THE GROUND.

HITMONTOP

PAGE 71

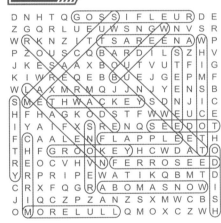

PAGE 72

VIBRAVA

FLAPPLE

AXEW

MUDBRAY

ELDEGOSS

SLIGGOO

THE 10 PURE GRASS-TYPE POKÉMON ARE CHERRIM, BOUNSWEET, GOSSIFLEUR, GROOKEY, LEAFEON, MARACTUS, SEEDOT, STEENEE, THWACKEY, TSAREENA

PAGE 73

DUSS KLOPSE:	DUSCLOPS
GA THO REE TA:	GOTHORITA
AWK TILL EERIE:	OCTILLERY
SHIE KNOT ICKE:	SHIINOTIC
CHREV IN IN T:	TREVENANT
WIM SIK OTT:	WHIMSICOTT

PAGE 74

ACCELGOR: BUG

STEENEE: GRASS

GLALIE: ICE

VAPOREON: WATER

DIGLETT: GROUND

ARCANINE: FIRE

GURDURR: FIGHTING

ELECTRIKE: ELECTRIC

KLANG: STEEL

PAGE 75

PAGE 76

A ROUGH CUSTOMER THAT WILDLY FLAILS ITS GIANT CLAWS. IT IS SAID TO BE EXTREMELY HARD TO RAISE.

CRAWDAUNT

PAGE 77

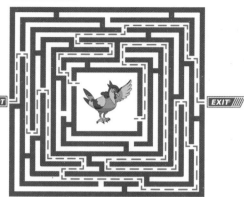

START

EXIT

PAGE 78

TOGEKISS

Answer: TOGEKISS

PAGE 79

4

PAGE 80

CHARJABUG:
BUG-ELECTRIC

JOLTIK:
BUG-ELECTRIC

VIKAVOLT:
BUG-ELECTRIC

SHELMET:
BUG

METAPOD:
BUG

GRUBBIN:
BUG

CATERPIE:
BUG

PIKACHU:
ELECTRIC

MANECTRIC:
ELECTRIC

JOLTEON:
ELECTRIC

PAGE 81

WOBBUFFET

MUNNA

PAGE 82

1. FALSE
2. TRUE
3. FALSE
4. TRUE
5. TRUE
6. FALSE
7. TRUE
8. FALSE
9. FALSE
10. TRUE

PAGE 84

NOY BATT:	NOIBAT
SNEEZE L:	SNEASEL
TIE RO GUH:	TYROGUE
VES PAH KWEEN:	VESPIQUEN
SKOR BUN EE:	SCORBUNNY
SQO VETTE:	SKWOVET
L KREEM EE:	ALCREMIE
AVE AL UGG:	AVALUGG
SHAN DA LEWER:	CHANDELURE
KOR FESH:	CORPHISH

PAGE 85

SNEASEL
STEALIX
BEARTIC
STERNATUS
TYROGUE

PAGE 86

RIBOMBEE
GALVANTULA
CINDERACE
RABOOT
INTELEON
TOGEKISS
THWACKEY
DRIZZILE

PAGE 88

ABLE TO CUT DOWN ANYTHING WITH A SINGLE STRIKE, IT BECAME KNOWN AS THE FAIRY KING'S SWORD AND IT INSPIRED AWE IN FRIEND AND FOE ALIKE.

ZACIAN

GALAR REGION POKÉMON HEIGHT AND WEIGHT CHART

Here's a handy reference chart for some of the tougher puzzles! Refer to the chart when you're stuck, or if you just want to brush up on some of the Pokémon living in the Galar region that we've discovered so far. Only the Pokémon found in this activity book are listed in this reference chart!

ALCREMIE
TYPE Fairy
HT 1' | WT 1.1 lbs.

CHANDELURE
TYPE Ghost-Fire
HT 3'3" | WT 75.6 lbs.

CINDERACE
TYPE Fire
HT 4'7" | WT 72.8 lbs.

CORVIKNIGHT
TYPE Flying-Steel
HT 7'3" | WT 165.3 lbs.

DRAMPA
TYPE Normal-Dragon
HT 9'10" | WT 407.9 lbs.

DURALUDON
TYPE Steel-Dragon
HT 5'11" | WT 88.2 lbs.

GALARIAN FARFETCH'D
TYPE Fighting
HT 2'7" | WT 92.6 lbs.

GOSSIFLEUR
TYPE Grass
HT 14" | WT 4.9 lbs.

ARAQUANID
TYPE Water-Bug
HT 5'11" | WT 180.8 lbs.

CHARIZARD
TYPE Fire-Flying
HT 5'7" | WT 199.5 lbs.

CHINCHOU
TYPE Water-Electric
HT 1'8" | WT 26.5 lbs.

CORVISQUIRE
TYPE Flying
HT 2'7" | WT 35.3 lbs.

DREDNAW
TYPE Water-Rock
HT 3'3" | WT 254.6 lbs.

ELDEGOSS
TYPE Grass
HT 1'8" | WT 5.5 lbs.

FLAPPLE
TYPE Grass-Dragon
HT 1' | WT 2.2 lbs.

GOURGEIST
TYPE Ghost-Grass
HT 2'11" | WT 27.6 lbs.

AVALUGG
TYPE Ice
HT 6'7" | WT 1113.3 lbs.

CHARJABUG
TYPE Bug-Electric
HT 1'8" | WT 23.1 lbs.

CINCCINO
TYPE Normal
HT 1'8" | WT 16.5 lbs.

CRAMORANT
TYPE Flying-Water
HT 2'7" | WT 39.7 lbs.

DRIZZILE
TYPE Water
HT 2'4" | WT 25.4 lbs.

ELECTRIKE
TYPE Electric
HT 2' | WT 33.5 lbs.

GARBODOR
TYPE Poison
HT 6'3" | WT 236.6 lbs.

GREEDENT
TYPE Normal
HT 2' | WT 13.2 lbs.

BEWEAR
TYPE Normal-Fighting
HT 6'11" | WT 297.6 lbs.

CHEWTLE
TYPE Water
HT 1' | WT 18.7 lbs.

COFAGRIGUS
TYPE Ghost
HT 5'7" | WT 168.7 lbs.

DITTO
TYPE Normal
HT 1' | WT 8.8 lbs.

DUBWOOL
TYPE Normal
HT 4'3" | WT 94.8 lbs.

ETERNATUS
TYPE Poison-Dragon
HT 65'7" | WT 2094.4 lbs.

GLOOM
TYPE Grass-Poison
HT 2'7" | WT 19 lbs.

GROOKEY
TYPE Grass
HT 1' | WT 11 lbs.

HAXORUS — TYPE: Dragon — HT: 5'11" — WT: 232.6 lbs.

MILCERY — TYPE: Fairy — HT: 8" — WT: 0.7 lbs.

MUNCHLAX — TYPE: Normal — HT: 2' — WT: 231.5 lbs.

QUAGSIRE — TYPE: Water-Ground — HT: 4'7" — WT: 165.3 lbs.

ROTOM — TYPE: Electric-Ghost — HT: 1' — WT: 0.7 lbs.

SILICOBRA — TYPE: Ground — HT: 7'3" — WT: 16.8 lbs.

STEELIX — TYPE: Steel-Ground — HT: 30'2" — WT: 881.8 lbs.

THWACKEY — TYPE: Grass — HT: 2'4" — WT: 30.9 lbs.

YAMPER — TYPE: Electric — HT: 1' — WT: 29.8 lbs.

INTELEON — TYPE: Water — HT: 6'3" — WT: 99.6 lbs.

MIMIKYU — TYPE: Ghost-Fairy — HT: 8" — WT: 1.5 lbs.

NICKIT — TYPE: Dark — HT: 2' — WT: 19.6 lbs.

RABOOT — TYPE: Fire — HT: 2' — WT: 19.8 lbs.

RUFFLET — TYPE: Normal-Flying — HT: 1'8" — WT: 23.1 lbs.

SKWOVET — TYPE: Normal — HT: 1' — WT: 5.5 lbs.

SUDOWOODO — TYPE: Rock — HT: 3'11" — WT: 83.8 lbs.

TOGEDEMARU — TYPE: Electric-Steel — HT: 1' — WT: 7.3 lbs.

ZACIAN — TYPE: Fairy-Steel — HT: 9'2" — WT: 782.6 lbs.

JOLTEON — TYPE: Electric — HT: 2'7" — WT: 54 lbs.

MORPEKO — TYPE: Electric-Dark — HT: 1' — WT: 6.6 lbs.

ORANGURU — TYPE: Normal-Psychic — HT: 4'11" — WT: 167.6 lbs.

RILLABOOM — TYPE: Grass — HT: 6'11" — WT: 198.4 lbs.

SCORBUNNY — TYPE: Fire — HT: 1' — WT: 9.9 lbs.

SNORLAX — TYPE: Normal — HT: 6'11" — WT: 1014.1 lbs.

SWINUB — TYPE: Ice-Ground — HT: 1'4" — WT: 14.3 lbs.

TYPE: NULL — TYPE: Normal — HT: 6'3" — WT: 265.7 lbs.

ZAMAZENTA — TYPE: Fighting-Steel — HT: 9'6" — WT: 1730.6 lbs.

MEOWSTIC (MALE) — TYPE: Psychic — HT: 2' — WT: 18.7 lbs.

MUDSDALE — TYPE: Ground — HT: 8'2" — WT: 2028.3 lbs.

GALARIAN PONYTA — TYPE: Psychic — HT: 2'7" — WT: 52.9 lbs.

ROOKIDEE — TYPE: Flying — HT: 8" — WT: 4 lbs.

SHUCKLE — TYPE: Bug-Rock — HT: 2' — WT: 45.2 lbs.

SOBBLE — TYPE: Water — HT: 1' — WT: 8.8 lbs.

SYLVEON — TYPE: Fairy — HT: 3'3" — WT: 51.8 lbs.

WOOLOO — TYPE: Normal — HT: 2' — WT: 13.2 lbs.